A special introduction by Jenny Nimmo
for *Hodder's April Story Book*

The Dragon's Child

When I realised that I could read on my own, and that in
between the covers of any book about any thing, lay
words that I could understand, it was as though a light
had been switched on. I had been living in the dark and,
all at once, my field of vision was extended to infinity.
I was an only, lonely child and a book became everything
to me: a refuge, an escape, an adventure, an entertainment,
an endless source of information, but more than anything,
a book became a friend.

Hodder
Children's
Books

a division of Hodder Headline plc

About the Author

Jenny Nimmo worked at the BBC for many years, ending in a spell as a director/adaptor for *Jackanory*, when she started writing her own stories. She is now the author of over twenty books for young people, including *The Snow Spider* – winner of the 1986 Smarties Book Prize. She lives in a converted watermill in Wales with her artist husband and three children.

Praise for *The Dragon's Child*

"It has a timeless, ageless quality in a once-upon-a-time-land . . . a gripping story"

TIMES LITERARY SUPPLEMENT

"Nimmo cannot fail to craft fiction that has a genuine sense of wonder . . . guaranteed to enthral this age range"

BOOKS FOR KEEPS

The Dragon's Child

JENNY NIMMO

Illustrated by Alan Marks

Hodder
Children's
Books

a division of Hodder Headline plc

Text copyright © 1977 Jenny Nimmo
Illustrations Copyright © 1997 Alan Marks

First published in Great Britain in 1997
by Hodder Children's Books

This paperback edition published in Great Britain
in 1999 by Hodder Children's Books

The right of Jenny Nimmo and Alan Marks to be identified as the
Author and Illustrator of the Work has been asserted by them in
accordance with the Copyright, Designs and Patents Act 1988.

10 9 8 7 6 5

A Catalogue record for this book is available from the
British Library

ISBN 0 340 75277 7

Printed and bound in Great Britain by
The Guernsey Press Co. Ltd., Vale, Guernsey, Channel Islands

Hodder Children's Books
A Division of Hodder Headline plc
338 Euston Road
London NW1 3BH

Contents

For Rose, Oliver and Daniel

Flying

On a deep cave beside the sea, a mother dragon watched her child trying to fly. It was hopeless. He was going about it in quite the wrong way. He would patter across the floor of the cave, leap, fall and skid on the wet sand.

"No, no, child," sighed the mother dragon. "Lift your wings, not your feet."

Her child had small, fragile wings, moth-like and silky. They were not ready to carry him aloft. And yet they had to. Time was running out. The dragon colony was moving on, and this time it was never coming back. Secretly, the dragon's mother held out little hope. Her child was too

young to fly. He had been born very late in the season. But what else could she do? She had to encourage him to try. Perhaps, a miracle would happen.

The little dragon tried again. This time he bumped into the cave wall and gave a squeal. His mother groaned but he gazed up at her with such sad yellow eyes, she couldn't be angry with him. Anger would make flames leap from her wide nostrils and the cave would glow with fierce colours; giant shadows would loom on the steaming walls and the little dragon would crawl into a corner and cry. He was afraid of fire and shadows, even his own. So his mother bent her neck until her nose was almost touching his, and she said, "Think flying, dear! Let your thoughts run into your wings."

"I've tried that," said the dragon's child, avoiding her eye, "but it doesn't work."

"Then we'll take a rest and go fishing." She tried to sound patient but her voice was beginning to take on a rather snappy

note, and she couldn't hold back the little jet of steam that shot out of her nose.

Her child jumped back squealing.

"Pull yourself together," grumbled his mother. "Sometimes I wonder if you're a dragon or a mouse." And the bridge of her nose crackled with the flames that she was only just managing to restrain.

Wounded by his mother's words, the dragon's child turned and ran out of the cave. If only he could practise flying in the open, he thought, he might be more successful. He knew why his mother wouldn't let him. She was ashamed, ashamed and embarrassed, because all the other dragon children had been flying for months. They were showing off all over the place, leaping from rocks, flying into trees, skimming the waves and even performing aerial acrobatics. "Look out stupid," they would call as their flying tails tickled his head. "Can't catch us!" they jeered as they soared into clouds of sea mist. The dragon's child felt left out and humiliated.

He moped along the edge of the tide, dragging his small tail through the surf, now and then thumping the ridges of wet sand. A bird began to follow him. She hopped beside his tail and then flew up and swooped round his head.

"Stop showing off!" snapped the little dragon.

The bird swung out in front of him and landed on the sand a few yards ahead. "I wasn't showing off," she said. "I thought you'd like some company."

"I'm rather pre-occupied," the dragon's child said loftily, "with my own thoughts."

"Can't you fly?" asked the bird, hopping sideways.

The dragon glanced at another child, wheeling joyfully above the rocks. "Not yet," he replied. "But I'm still very young. I was the last dragon to be born. One day soon I'll fly."

"Flying isn't always the answer," said the bird. "My parents could fly, but it didn't save them. They would have been better off breathing fire."

The dragon's child noticed that the bird was also very young. Was she an orphan? He couldn't imagine what life would be like without a mother. "What happened to your parents?" he asked.

"Doggins," the bird whispered.

"Doggins?" The dragon's child sat down with a thump. "Doggins?" The very word struck fear into the heart of every creature. Even dragons feared doggins, feared and loathed them, for doggins were wicked animals, utterly without honour. They killed without reason, hunting in packs, not for survival but for fun. They liked nothing so much as a game of catch and torment. Their bodies were muscled machines, covered in short grey hair, their shape owing more to a panther than a wolf. Their eyes were red dots of fire, and their long, naked noses drooped over awesome, razor-sharp teeth. Their most deadly weapons, however, were their tails, long, hairless cords which they whipped round small creatures before swallowing them whole.

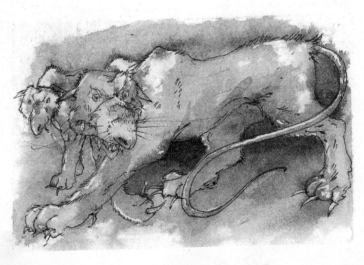

And even though they were afraid of fire, they would leap on a dragon's back all together and bite him, before his flames could reach them.

The dragon's child had heard of these terrible battles. His own grandfather, the great Emperor Dando, had been killed in this way. It was an outrage. There had been such a storm of grief-stricken fury the sky had turned red for a whole season, the sea had become a boiling cauldron and the doggins' forest homes had been burned to the ground. The doggins that survived the fires had retreated deep, deep in to the forest. They hadn't been seen since.

"Are they back, then?" asked the dragon's child. "Are they here? Near our caves? In the trees?" He looked round fearfully.

"I don't know where they are now," said the bird. "A month ago, when my mother and I were sleeping on the cliffs, my father woke us with a scream. 'Doggins! Doggins!' he cried. My mother flew into the air, perhaps to lead them away and save me. But she never came back, nor did my father. It was so cold in the nest without them."

"Can doggins fly, then?" asked the little dragon, aghast.

"No. But when a bird swoops low, the doggins catch it with their terrible tails."

"That's bad," said the dragon's child. "Horrible." He raced back to the cave, imagining the thunder of wicked feet behind him, and a draught of mad, savage breath on his neck. He tore into the cave with the dreadful name on his tongue, "Doggins! Doggins! Doggins!"

"What?" cried his mother. "Where? Here?"

"Not exactly," confessed the little dragon. "But soon, perhaps." And he told her about the orphaned bird.

"It's just as well we're leaving tomorrow," she said.

"Tomorrow?" Her child looked up with a mouth that gaped so wide it showed every one of his small, useless (at present) teeth.

"Dragons always fly back to their Homeland in summer. I've told you before."

"But tomorrow?" said her child. "I didn't know it would be so soon." He glanced nervously at his wings. "Tell me again about the Homeland, and how we find it."

His mother considered a moment, and then she answered, "The Homeland is everlasting brightness. It's pure and cool and always safe. And a dragon can find it without searching, for its tug on your heart is so strong you cannot escape it." She smiled to herself and as she continued she

16

didn't notice her child's expression of wonder beginning to fade. "We all take off together," she said, "we soar through the clouds in a beautiful pattern, like the tail of a flying fish. I believe it's quite a spectacle."

"But mother," said the little dragon, "I can't fly."

"Oh," she said, suddenly remembering. "Nor can you. Yet."

"What shall I do?" Her child's voice rose to a wail.

"Practice," she told him. "It's now or never."

So the dragon's child practised all night. He bumped and jumped, skidded and rolled until his exhausted mother fell asleep. Her gentle snores steamed into the cave and beads of moisture glittered on the moonlit walls. And still the little dragon jumped and leapt, until every part of him was bruised and aching, while on a ledge above the cave, the orphaned bird listened to his efforts, wondering how she could help him.

Next morning, when the sun beamed across the ocean, the mother dragon and her child were still fast asleep. But the bird had been awake since first light. The tall cliffs echoed with the slap and thrash of waves and the scream of sea birds.

The bird stood up and preened her feathers, and as she did so, something caught her sharp eye. Far, far out a dark shape moved on the horizon. The bird watched, motionless; she had never seen a ship, never heard of one, but her fragile bones rang with fear and she uttered her first warning call, a sound she had learned from her parents. For she knew that this dark thing, riding the ocean, carried something just as dangerous as doggins.

Strangers from the Sea

When he woke up, the dragon's child was so weary his mother didn't have the heart to make him practise flying again.

"Today you must rest," she said. "You're obviously too tired to try flying. The colony will have to leave without us. Perhaps, tomorrow you'll be able to fly. Now go and lie in the sun or roll in the sea. The salt water will heal your bruises."

They sat together on the beach while the other dragons began to make ready for the long journey north. The noise was deafening. Young dragons shrieked with excitement, teenagers argued, fathers stormed over the cliffs barking out orders, while mothers whirled about, calling their children and calming the elderly.

As the dragon's child gazed round at the commotion, his mother nudged him gently and said, "Your father's coming this way."

A tremor rippled over the sand as the great dragon approached. The little dragon's tender spines prickled with alarm.

"Don't show your fear," his mother whispered. "Prince Kai looks for spirit and determination in his children."

So the little dragon stood as tall as he could and squinted up into Prince Kai's golden eyes, even though they were so far above him they were almost out of sight.

"I've come to give my youngest child courage before the long flight," boomed Prince Kai.

The mother dragon coughed and said, "Actually, we'll be travelling tomorrow, dear, or the day after."

"How is that?" Prince Kai demanded. Before his mother could explain, the little dragon piped up, "I can't fly – yet."

"I see." The huge dragon's eyebrows shot up, and he stared thoughtfully at his smallest child. "You realise I have to go to-day. I am the leader. I can't alter my plans just for you!"

"I understand," said the dragon's child in a steady voice.

His mother felt proud of him. "Before you go, my dear," she said to Prince Kai, "how about giving our child a name? I just can't think of one."

"Mm!" snorted the big dragon, and for several seconds he studied his child very carefully. "Dando!" he declared, at last.

"Dando?" echoed the mother dragon. "But that is . . . that *was* an Emperor's name. Dando-the-fearless, the-most excellent, the-incomparable . . ."

"And I can't even fly," the child reminded his father. "I don't deserve such a splendid name."

"Then earn it," boomed the big dragon and he wheeled round, his great tail sweeping a pile of sand into the air and letting it fall in a golden shower all over his youngest child.

"I . . . ashoo . . . will!" sneezed the little dragon.

Prince Kai looked over his scaly shoulder, "Fly soon, my son," he called "because we're leaving this land for good. These are troubled times, and we're never coming back."

22

The other dragons were by now assembled on the cliff top. As soon as Prince Kai joined them, they rose in the air and soared over the ocean. Their great wings fanned the waves into towers of spray, and as they flew, higher and higher, it seemed as though the clouds were swallowing a mighty fishtail, a fishtail that had a tiny bite taken out of it, the place where the dragon and her child should have been. And the little dragon felt a stab of dread when he saw the empty cliffs and heard nothing but silence in the air. For a great many birds had travelled north with the dragons. And it seemed such a lonely place without the comforting chorus of musical voices.

But the orphan bird had stayed behind and that night, while the dragon and her child slept, she watched the moonlit ocean from her roost above the cave, and she saw a dark shadow slide closer over the water, taking the shape of a long hollow tree. And she saw startling pale clouds billow out above the tree, and the movement of creatures inside it. The bird eyed the strange craft with dismay, but she managed to keep her fear to herself until dawn, when all at once, she opened her beak and let out a shrill call of alarm. "Strangers on the sea!" she cried. "Strangers on the sea!"

The dragon and her child woke up and rushed out on to the sand. "What is it?" cried the little dragon when he saw the billowing sails and the dark hull crashing through the surf.

"Humans!" said his mother in a voice that rumbled with agitation.

"What are they?"

"As bad as doggins if not worse," she said. "You will have to fly now, child. There is no other way!" She tore across the sand with her child shambling after her, and when they rounded an outcrop of weed covered rocks, she said, "Here you must practise, out of sight, until you can fly."

The dragon's child leapt and tumbled. He willed strength into his feeble wings. He told himself to, "Fly – soar – lift – swing," and once he found himself skimming the ground, almost airborne. Once, he even bounced as high as his mother's nose. But he couldn't fly.

His mother began to panic. What can I do? she thought. She hummed to herself trying to cover her agitation. She couldn't desert her child, but suppose he never learned to fly? And then it came to her. Once a mother dragon had carried her child on the long migration. But the child had been smaller than this one. Would it be safe? "I'll have to carry you," she said, rather breathlessly.

"Carry?" piped her child. "How? In your mouth? In your claws?"

"No, no!" she said. "On my back. But you must hold fast to my spines and don't let go whatever happens. This is a dangerous thing to attempt. Are you ready?"

"Ready? Ready?" her child squeaked nervously. "I suppose I am. I suppose it's now or never."

"Now or never," said his mother, and she knelt on the sand while her child tried to climb on to her back. It wasn't easy. Her scales were hard and shiny, and her spines cut into the soft pads of his feet. As her great body lifted into the air, the little dragon's stomach lurched, the cold wind thundered in his skull and froze his nose and ears. He closed his eyes and clung on tight, but slowly, slowly his mother's spines slipped out of his grasp.

"I can't hold on," he cried, but the wind smothered his voice. "Mother, I'm falling," he screamed, but his mother couldn't feel the small tumbling body through her thick shiny scales.

With a final squeal, the dragon's child slid from his mother's back and fell earthwards through the wind. And the beat of her great wings drowned his fading calls. "Mother! Mother!"

We're flying home, she thought.
Unaware that her child was gone.

The Prisoner

When the bird saw the dragon and her child soar into the sky she flew after them. She didn't want to be left alone. She had almost caught up with the great flying dragon when, to her horror, she saw the child slip from his mother's back and fall towards the ground. The big dragon hadn't seemed to notice.

"Your child is gone!" shrieked the bird. But she couldn't get close enough to be heard. The swirl of air around the dragon's huge wings beat her back. I can't leave the little dragon all alone, thought the bird. Something terrible could happen to him. Doggins are creeping through the forest and the strangers on the sea are getting closer.

So the bird turned back and flew over the stretch of bracken where she had seen the little dragon fall. "Dragon's child!" she called. "Dragon's child, are you hurt?"

Fortunately, the bracken had softened the little dragon's fall, and although he was bruised and dizzy, he wasn't injured. "Is my mother coming back?" he asked.

The bird flew down and perched beside him. "I don't think she knows that you fell," she said gently. "Maybe she won't find out until the end of her journey."

"Ooooo!" wailed the little dragon.

"I won't leave you," the bird said. "I know what it's like to be alone. You just try and stay hidden until dark, for the creatures on the water are heading this way, and who knows what they may do?"

The little dragon shuddered. "My mother called them humans," he said, and crept deeper into the bracken, screwing his eyes up tight against the things that would crawl out of the sea. He had never felt so frightened or alone.

The bird flew up to the highest point on the cliffs and watched the mysterious craft. Before it reached the beach it stopped moving, and the creatures inside leapt into the sea. They were very noisy these humans, they shouted and splashed through the water in a clumsy and untidy way. When they ran onto the beach they kicked at the sand and jostled each other.

They wore gleaming jackets of ribbed metal and beneath their silvery helmets their thick white hair hung in long plaited tails. All except one, who was bare headed and dressed in scarlet. She was much smaller than the others, yet the bundle she carried was so heavy it caused her to stumble and sway. A woman with a wide, stern face kept barking orders at her, and the girl frowned with the effort of trying to keep up.

The band of humans began to climb the cliff, never guessing that dragons' tails had swept the path they walked or that a dragon was hiding so close. When they reached the top they swarmed over the bracken, making for the edge of the forest where they would build a new town.

The bird flew this way and that, trying to lead the humans away from the place where the little dragon was hiding. But the humans took no notice. Only the girl guessed what the bird was doing, and she kept her eyes on the ground, looking for a nest or a clutch of eggs. When the woman she followed stopped for a moment's rest, the girl found herself gazing into the shadows beneath a patch of leaves, and there she made out the shape of a small curled-up creature. At that moment the dragon's child raised his head, and his gleaming yellow-gold eyes found hers. The girl suddenly felt such an intense happiness she couldn't stop herself from smiling. She had never seen a dragon but from her father's descriptions she knew immediately that she was looking at one. She also knew that she must keep the secret to herself. Dragons were mysterious and sacred creatures; they must never be allowed to fall into the hands of an enemy. And these big white haired people who had taken her prisoner, were everybody's enemies.

"Manon! What are you gazing at?" shouted the stern faced woman. Her name was Lady Bolda, and she was the wife of Great Smould, leader of the Welkin people, so she thought herself very important.

"Nothing, Lady Bolda." Manon turned her smile into a stupid grin, and no one guessed that she had seen something wonderful, even when she began to hum the tune her family used to sing on days of celebration.

But the boy called Lord Drum didn't like Manon's humming. Round his neck he wore a big tin drum, hanging by a cord, and all day long he would beat the tin with two wooden sticks. The Welkin people were not musical, but no one told him to stop. No one seemed to mind. Besides, Lord Drum was Great Smould's only son.

The boy came leaping up behind Manon. "I don't like the sound you're making," he shouted.

"Too bad," said Manon, under her breath.

"What's that? What are you saying?"

Manon had learnt Lord Drum's language, but he couldn't understand hers. "I said I'm sorry. Sorry, Lord Drum."

He stared at her, suspiciously. Was she teasing him? He couldn't tell. They were the only children in the group but they couldn't play together. Manon was a prisoner and he was Lord Drum, son of Great Smould.

He wandered away. Boom! Boom! Rat-a-tat! Boom! went the big tin drum. When he was out of earshot Manon began to hum again. She couldn't help it. She felt sure the dragon was a lucky omen.

That evening Lady Bolda sent Manon to gather twigs from the forest. Alone among the giant trees, Manon's excitement bubbled up and spilled out in joyful singing. The bird, circling above the trees, was astonished to hear the girl with the sad face making such happy sounds; and Lord Drum, hiding at the edge of the forest, wondered what had happened to make the little prisoner suddenly so cheerful.

Deep in the trees, other creatures heard Manon singing; creatures with coarse grey hair and long tough tails, creatures that hated singing. But they crept closer, thinking that the singing thing might be good to eat.

When Manon had collected an armful of twigs, she laid them on the bonfire. A camp had already begun to take shape around the fire. The dwellings were flimsy shelters made with metal frames and silky, shiny cloth, but tomorrow the real building would take place, and Manon sighed, thinking of the boulders she would have to carry up from the beach.

The people had found plenty of food to roast: rabbits, fish and sea-birds were turning on the spit. Manon sat at the edge of the circle waiting for Lady Bolda to throw her a few scraps. The long journey had made her very hungry, and it was all she could do to stop herself rushing in and grabbing at food like the others.

The fire threw glittering sparks into the black sky, and Manon watched them cascade back to earth like falling stars. Long before they touched the bracken, the damp night wind had blown them out. Only two sparks still glowed, like tiny round lamps. The dragon's child had caught scent of the food and, desperately hungry, he had come closer to the campfire.

"Dragon, go away!" whispered Manon. "There's danger here. Go! Quickly. Before they catch you!"

"What are you saying?" hissed Lord Drum. "And who are you talking to? Tell me, or you won't get any food."

"I'm talking to myself," said Manon.

"I don't believe you!" he pushed his face close to hers. "I think you've got a little pet hidden somewhere. If you have, it had better watch out, because I shall catch it!"

Manon Meets a Dragon

The dragon's child drew back into the undergrowth, his ears tingling. The boy with the tin drum frightened him. What was he saying to make the girl look so alarmed?

Dando raced to the beach and when he reached the cave, he flung himself on his favourite rock and lay, full-stretch in the safe, damp darkness of home. There he snuffled and moaned and sobbed big tragic tears of hunger and fear and loneliness, reliving every moment of the whole dreadful day. But, all at once, he remembered something so strange that it made him stop crying.

"I understood," he said to himself. "The human spoke and I understood."

Was it the girl's anxious face, or her hushed, tense voice? No it wasn't that. It was her language. Every word she had spoken meant something to him. Go. Quick. Danger. Catch. And – dragon. That's what he was. Dando the dragon.

He sat up and stared into the darkness marvelling at the extraordinary thing that had happened. Dragons understood the language of birds, they always had, but humans? Surely not. There was something special about the girl, special about them both.

Dando closed his eyes and curled himself comfortably on his favourite rock. Too tired to think about the questions spinning in his head, he fell asleep and dreamed he was flying, all by himself.

"Wake up, dragon's child!" The bird hopped into the cave. Morning light flooded the beach behind her. "You can't sleep all day."

Dando opened his eyes. He couldn't think why he was so tired and so sad. And then he remembered. "My mother's gone. I'm all alone."

"No you're not. You've got me," the bird said fiercely. "And you're going to be fine, aren't you dragon's child?"

41

The dragon sat up. "I am," he agreed, "I'm Dando – I'm a dragon and last night something amazing happened to me." And he told the bird all about the girl who spoke a language he understood.

The bird was impressed. "But you shouldn't have gone so near to humans," she warned. "Imagine what would have happened if they'd caught you."

"I can't," said the dragon's child. "What would they have done with me do you think?"

"I daren't think," the bird replied. "It's too scary."

"That bad?" Dando slipped off his favourite rock. "I'm hungry," he announced. "Where shall I get breakfast?" He was thinking of the camp fire and the delicious smell of roasting.

"We'll catch a fish. Come with me!" The bird flew across the sand and began to skim the water. Her bright eye caught a movement under the waves and down she plunged. When she bobbed up on the surf, she held a bright silvery fish in her beak. Dando watched the bird swoop off the sea and land on the sand. She laid the fish before him. "We'll share it," she said.

But Dando had lost his appetite. "I can't." He stared miserably at the fish. "It's yours. I shall never be able to catch my own breakfast because I can't fly."

"You can swim," offered the bird. "Of course you'll be able to catch your own breakfast. Now eat up. You're going to need all the strength you can get, because after breakfast, I'm going to teach you how to fly."

The dragon's child let out such a sigh it ruffled the bird's feathers. Luckily, his breath was still quite free of fire, but the bird took care not to stand too close to him while they ate their breakfast.

After the meal, flying lessons began. The bird was a good teacher, kind and patient, but she began to get cross when the dragon's child showed no sign at all of becoming airborne. He seemed to have lost heart, and she suspected that he wasn't even trying to spread his wings. "Dragon's child, I'm fed up," the bird said, at last. "I don't believe you're interested in flying."

Dando seemed not to hear her. He was gazing over the bird's head. She hopped round and saw a girl, with her arms full of seaweed, walking through the shallow pools that sparkled at the edge of the sea.

At the same moment the girl saw the dragon's child. She dropped her seaweed and stood motionless, while the tide lapped round her ankles. The bird lifted into the air with fright. "Look out!" she called to the dragon's child, and flew up to a safe hollow in the cliff.

Dando took no notice. He felt as though he were under a spell. Slowly, the girl began to approach him. He stood his ground, listening to his thumping heart and watching the girl, every step of the way, as she moved closer and closer. And then, he found that he was moving too, very slowly, as if the girl were tugging him by a strong and invisible thread.

The bird could hardly believe her eyes. "Oh dear! Oh dear! Oh dear!" she cried. "What's going to happen? This is wrong, all wrong."

The dragon's child was now in the girl's shadow, less than an arm's length away. She bent down and touched his head. "A dragon," she whispered. "A real dragon!"

Dando grunted with pleasure, turning his head under her gentle fingers. It felt so good to be stroked like this.

When the girl put both arms round him, he didn't move, and when she lifted him up and cradled him like a baby, he just closed his eyes and gave a happy little sigh.

"No! No! No!" screamed the bird. She swept down from the cliff and round the girl's head, crying, "Run away, dragon's child. This is dangerous. I'm your friend. I know."

The dragon's child ignored the bird. He felt very comfortable. This was almost as good as cuddling close to his mother.

The bird was making such a noise, none of them heard the drum until it came, "Boom-boom. Rat-a-tat, boom," down the cliff path.

"Lord Drum," gasped Manon. "He mustn't find you." She looked round the beach searching for somewhere to hide. When she saw the cave she rushed into it and hid in the deep shadows behind the dragon's favourite rock. The bird flew up to her perch, high on the cliff, where she worried and worried, screaming and squawking.

"Rat-a-tat! Boom! Rat-a-tat! Boom!" Lord Drum marched over the sand.

"Little dragon, don't make a sound,"

whispered Manon. "Lord Drum mustn't find us."

But on he came "Rat-a-tat! Boom! Rat-a-tat! Boom!" He walked into the cave and, squinting through the darkness, spied a girl crouching behind a rock.

"So there you are, Manon," said Lord Drum "What are you doing?"

"Nothing, Lord Drum." Manon knelt in the sand, trying to hide the little dragon.

"You're hiding something." Lord Drum stepped closer. "What is it?"

"Nothing," said Manon. "Nothing special."

"Ah, but I think it is," said Lord Drum. "I think it's something very special and I'm going to get it!" And he beat a long, threatening roll on his drum.

Catching a Fabulous Beast

"Run, little dragon! Run as fast as you can!" cried Manon.

The dragon leapt out of her arms. He rushed to the mouth of the cave, past the drummer, and out on to the shining sand, bleating for his mother in a high, terrified voice, a voice that she would never hear.

The bird swooped down from the cliff, scolding the dragon's child with piercing shrieks. "Silly little dragon," she called. "Didn't I tell you to beware of people? Didn't I tell you not to trust them?" She swung away as Lord Drum came speeding towards them.

Dando raced for the cliff path, his heart pounding as loud and as fast as the drum beats behind him, and as he stumbled up the cliff, the bird tilted in the sky above him, calling, "Hide, little dragon. Hide where they can't find you!"

This had already occurred to Dando and as soon as he reached the cliff-top he darted under the nearest clump of leaves. The bracken gave excellent cover and he wriggled along in the tunnels beneath a sea of broad leaves, without ruffling the surface at all.

But Lord Drum wouldn't give up. "I'll get you! I'll get you!" he cried. Manon, racing behind him, called out, "Please don't hurt him, Lord Drum, just leave him, he's only a . . . a . . ."

"A what?" demanded the drumming boy. "What is he, Manon? Tell me."

She would never tell. She would rather die. "Just a poor little creature, that won't do you any harm," she said.

"Don't lie to me, Manon!" he snorted. "It's a fabulous creature. Something magical and special, and I want it." And

he raced back to camp crying, "Come and
help me. Come and join in the hunt. I've
found a fabulous beast!"

Great Smould was admiring the shining
pavilion his people had built for him.
"Stop bothering us," he said "Go and play
somewhere else."

"I'm not playing," Lord Drum stamped
his foot. "I've seen a fabulous beast. We
must catch it, or it'll creep up at night and
eat us."

"Better do as the boy says," advised Lady Bolda. "I sense a tantrum coming on. Besides, he could be telling the truth."

"Very well," said Great Smould. "Describe this beast for us, young Drum."

"It has coppery-green scales, and golden eyes and a row of shiny spikes, no . . . triangles all along its back, and a long twisty tail that ends in a point like an arrowhead." Lord Drum looked so earnest, his father began to believe him.

"Hmm." Great Smould pulled at the ice-white whiskers on his long chin. Then he clapped his hands and called for attention. When his people had gathered round him, he said, "My son has seen a fabulous beast. It is obviously something we cannot allow to roam freely about our camp. It must be hunted down and caught before nightfall." He called upon his son once more to describe the beast he had seen, and the people listened intently to Lord Drum's story, which was embellished with the expressive thunder of his drumming.

Outside the circle, Manon heard an account of a creature she barely recognised, for Lord Drum made it sound as though the dragon's child was as big as a lion, when it would have been more accurate to say he was the size of a dog. They'll never find him, she thought. For they'll be searching for something quite different from a little dragon.

But Great Smould's people were not the sort to give up. They beat the bracken, scoured the cliffs and swept all the caves, they even explored the dark and dangerous forest, as far as they dared, poking in bushes, climbing trees and worrying bees with their nets of silvery steel. All this time the dragon's child hid in the bracken, scurrying this way and that, as sticks and brushes and beaters drew closer. It was only a matter of time, he realised, before all the bracken was flat and there was nowhere left for him to hide.

The bird screamed round the searchers' heads, not knowing what to do for the best. Should she try to lead them away, or pull their hair and peck at their noses! Lord Drum had a tantrum coming on and the bird made it worse. He dropped his net, picked up a rock and took aim. But before he could let it fly, a hand shot out and knocked the rock from his fist. Lord Drum whirled round and saw Manon running away. "You wretch," he yelled. "You stupid crazy thing!" He stormed after her and, leaping on the girl, brought her crashing to the ground.

"You're a bully!" cried Manon, pulling his hair. "A bully and a coward. You only fight things that are smaller than you are."

"I'm not a coward!" screamed the boy, but Manon kicked and scratched and bit and pummelled until Lord Drum had had enough. He jumped up, just managing to hold back a tide of furious tears.

Manon was about to make her escape when a voice called, "I've found it! I've found the fabulous beast!"

The dragon's child crouched in a sea of crushed stems. He stared out at the people with big golden eyes, hiding his fear and trying to be the dragon his father had commanded, trying to be worthy of the name he'd been given. Desperately, he searched for a way of escape, but the circle of people was closing around him.

"Run! Run! Run!" came Manon's voice. "It's not too late."

But it was. "He's mine!" screeched Lord Drum, and down came the big silver net. It fell over Dando before he had time to think. He gave a little wail of astonishment and dread, while Lord Drum laughed and beat out a roll of victory.

Night fell as they carried the dragon's child back to camp. They put him in a cage that swung from a long steel pole, and he lay with his tail curled up tight round his copper-green body, so still he might have been dead.

Manon kept close to the swinging cage, trying to reach the dragon with comforting whispers. "Don't be afraid. I'll save you! I promise!"

How could she? She was so much smaller than the Welkin people. They were tall and very strong; their deep, monotonous voices were terrifying to the little dragon, and he tried to banish the sounds from his head. But he couldn't stop himself from watching his captors, and his golden eyes blazed with the mirrored light of their flaming torches.

Lord Drum

They hung the cage in Great Smould's shining pavilion. The sun blazed through the glassy dome and the dragon's child had nowhere to shelter. His glowing scales became dull and dry, and beneath drooping eyelids his golden eyes mirrored nothing at all.

Lady Bolda was proud of her fabulous beast. "Come and see what my son has caught," she would boast to the other women. But they had lost their children on the long journeys through the air, the mountains and the sea. They had no sons to bring them fabulous beasts, so they were jealous of Lady Bolda and didn't pay much attention to the little dragon.

Sometimes, Lord Drum would come and gaze at his prize. He would poke sticks through the bars of the cage to make the little creature growl, and he beat his drum under the cage, sending the dragon whirling round his prison in a frenzy. Soon he growled and hissed whenever the boy appeared. And Lord Drum grew tired of his games. He wished the fabulous beast would like him, just a bit. Suddenly it was no fun being growled at all the time.

Manon was made to do the very thing she had most dreaded. Great Smould wanted a winter palace and all day she had to carry heavy boulders up from the beach. But in the evenings when Great Smould sat with his people round the fire, Manon would creep close to the pavilion and whisper through its thin walls, "Dragon! Dragon! Don't give up hope. I'll save you, somehow, I promise."

She didn't know how she could keep her promise. All day she was under the eyes of the Welkin people, and at night Great Smould and his wife slept right beside the dragon's cage. And then, one day, Great Smould ordered a grand feast to celebrate his son's birthday. That night the Welkin people danced round the fire, chanting their strange monotonous songs, and no one noticed Manon creep into the shining pavilion.

She ran straight to the dragon's cage, whispering, "I've come to save you, little dragon." She was shocked to see how thin and weak he had become. The door of the cage was padlocked, she hadn't expected that. She scratched and shook the big lock, but it was no use. She needed the key that hung from a chain round Lord Drum's neck. Perhaps she could steal it while he was asleep.

But if Manon couldn't rescue Dando, she could at least comfort him. She put her hand through the bars and stroked the soft scales on Dando's head. "I'll try and rescue you tonight," she whispered.

Dando looked up and sighed. He moved closer to the bars and breathed, "It may be too late. I think I am dying."

It was the first time the dragon had spoken to Manon and she was amazed when she realised that they could understand eachother's language. "I won't let you die," she said. "It's my fault that you're here. If I hadn't found you, Lord Drum would never have caught you."

"In time I would have been caught," the little dragon said. "I can't fly, you see. And a dragon that can't fly is no use at all."

"You are a magical creature," Manon said fiercely. "Believe in yourself and you will escape. I know it." She put her arm through the bars and hugged the little dragon tight. And Dando was so comforted he gave a faint but cheerful bleat.

Before Manon tiptoed away, the little dragon said, "Find the bird. She will help."

From the shadows outside, Lord Drum had watched the girl and the dragon. He wanted to jump in and frighten them, but he found that he couldn't. He couldn't even beat his drum. His hands fell to his sides and an ache that he didn't understand made him turn away in silence. He found that his drum didn't comfort him, nor did the dancing and chanting people. He went and lay under the quilt his mother had made from silk and feathers, and he turned his face to the wall. When Great Smould came to bid his son good night, he saw a tear shining on Lord Drum's face.

"What's this?" Great Smould peered at

his son. "Tears on
your birthday,
young Drum.
What's the matter?"

"I don't know,"
murmured Lord Drum.

"Then, why are
you crying?"

"Because I'm not Manon," sighed the boy.

"I can't believe my ears. You want to be a prisoner? An orphan? You're mad, boy. You must have eaten mouldy mushrooms."

"I haven't," whispered Lord Drum. But he couldn't explain why he felt so bad.

Next day he wandered about without his drum, and the absence of Lord Drum's constant "Rat-a-tat! Boom!" left a strange emptiness in the air. The people wondered what had happened to the one and only Welkin child. "Is he sick?" they asked his mother. "He looks so downcast."

"Why don't you play your drum?" Lady Bolda asked her son. "It would cheer you up."

"No it wouldn't," the boy replied. "I'm sick of my drum."

He went to the shining pavilion and looked in on the dragon's child. The little creature hardly moved. He lay in a miserable huddle, his eyes closed against the world. But when Lord Drum approached a warning rumble came from the cage.

"I won't hurt you," said Lord Drum. "I'd open the door of the cage, if you'd let me stroke you." And he held up the key that hung from a chain round his neck.

The dragon's child opened one eye and snarled at the boy.

"You hate me don't you?" cried Lord Drum. "So I'll never let you go. Never, never, never." And he rushed out of the pavilion and into the dark forest. And when he thought no one could hear him, he howled and howled out his pain and his fury, although he still couldn't understand what it was. Then he tore the key from his neck, and flung it into the shadowy depths of the forest.

Deep in the trees the doggins heard the terrible howling, and saw a flash of gold as the flying key was caught in a sunbeam. They wondered what it could be.

"Soon," they growled. "Soon." And they settled into their dens and waited.

Flames at Last

When Manon saw that the key round Lord Drum's neck had gone, she wondered where he had hidden it. She knew it was useless to ask. What can I do now? she thought, and then she remembered that the dragon had told her to find a bird. It seemed to be the dragon's friend. Perhaps it could help. But how would she find it? There were other birds who hadn't migrated, all with white and pearl-grey feathers.

"I'll just have to guess," Manon said to herself.

She worked very hard all morning and then she sat on the cliff-top and, using a tone she hoped a bird would find friendly, she called, "Friend of the dragon, are you here?"

The sea birds took no notice, they carried on fishing and flying, swimming and dozing, as if no one had spoken.

"I rescued a bird," Manon went on, "So one of you owes me a life. You could at least listen."

Birds swooped and called, and swung and fluttered, paying no attention to the girl on the cliff, all except one, sitting on a ledge just below her. It shuffled uneasily and turned its head.

"It's you," said Manon, "I know it is. So don't turn away."

The bird hunched itself into pearl-grey feathers and gave a soft gurgle.

"It's no use," said Manon. "You can't ignore me, and even if you don't understand every word, because you're a bird not a dragon, I know you'll get my meaning. Are you listening?"

The bird didn't understand her language but, somehow, she caught the drift of an urgent message. She knew the girl was talking about the dragon's child.

"I expect you think it's my fault the little dragon was caught, and in a way that's true, but you have to realise how I was feeling at the time." She leant closer to the bird. "When the Welkin people captured me I thought that I would never come close to happiness again. I don't know what happened to my parents the night we were invaded, I just woke up to find they had vanished. Maybe they were captured – maybe not. I think my people have probably ceased to exist. I'm afraid I'm the only one left." Manon glanced at the bird to see if her words were having any effect, but the bird had closed her eyes.

Manon sighed. Was the bird listening? It didn't really matter. She needed to tell her story even if no one heard it. "We knew the Welkins were coming but we couldn't stop them. They came from the sky, from another world, but their airship was blown up in battle, and now they're trapped on earth until they can find a way to build another. I think my father guessed what was going to happen. That's why he told me about dragons, so if I survived they wouldn't be forgotten. He said they'd all flown away and the world would never be the same, because dragons were the last marvels, the only creatures that could speak and understand our language, the only ones that still held magic. So when I saw a dragon, well, it gave me hope. There's a bit of magic left, I thought, even if it's very small. But now the little dragon's in a cage, and he'll die there unless we rescue him." This time Manon stared hard at the bird, and the bird looked right back at her and gave a wheezy sort of twitter.

"There's no one else, is there?" said Manon. "Just you and me. So we'd better get on with it." She got to her feet and waited to see what the bird would do. It didn't move.

Manon gazed sadly at the motionless form. "I suppose you are the wrong one," she said under her breath, "I thought you were the dragon's friend." And she began to walk away, wondering how she could rescue the dragon all by herself.

There was a movement in the air above her, and she looked up to see the bird swinging through the sky, almost as though it were laughing at having tricked her.

"You didn't fool me," Manon cried happily. "I knew it was you, all the time," and she ran back to the camp, with the bird swooping and gliding beside her. When they reached the shining pavilion the bird flew straight in, perched on the dragon's cage and set it swinging.

Too tired to open his eyes, the little dragon sensed the gentle motion and hoped he wasn't about to be tormented. "Go away." His growl was a faint little wheeze and it made the bird's feathers stand on end.

"What has happened to you, dragon's child?" she exclaimed.

The dragon's child opened his eyes and sat up. "Orphan bird, she found you then," he said, and his eyes held some of their old glitter. "I thought they'd caught or killed you."

"Not me," said the bird, forgetting to mention that Manon had saved her. "Dragon's child, you're not looking very good. You should be flying by now, or breathing fire at the least. We'll have to get you out of there."

The dragon's child sighed. "Tell me how," he asked. "I know you're a clever bird."

At that moment Lady Bolda walked in. Manon was trapped. "What are you doing?" screamed the woman. "I'll tie you up if I find you in here again."

Manon should have run away while she had the chance, but instead she put a hand on the dragon's cage and said, "Couldn't you let him out, just for a while, to stretch his legs. Your fabulous beast will die if you don't take better care of him."

"How dare you tell me what to do!" Lady Bolda cried, rushing at Manon in a rage. But Manon ducked out of reach and ran round the cage. The bird, in a panic, flew up to the blue sky she could see through the glass dome, but she smashed against its transparent panes and fell to earth in a fluttering tumble of feathers.

The dragon's child stared out on a scene that troubled and bewildered him. His friends were in danger and he couldn't reach them, couldn't help them. Anger began to simmer inside him, a fiery heat tickled his nostrils, and when he sneezed a tiny spark flew out and settled on Lady Bolda's arm.

"Ouch!" she screamed, her anger boiling into a storm of fury. Catching hold of Manon she shook the girl until poor Manon cried out for pity.

Shaking the dizziness out of her head, the bird swept herself up and flew to Manon's rescue, only to be knocked back by Lady Bolda's angry fist.

"What's this? What's this?" Great Smould strode into the shining pavilion. But before he could lift a finger, a long tongue of flame shot through the bars of the dragon's cage and he reeled back in astonishment.

"Dragon's child, you're breathing fire." The bird circled the glassy dome, crying, "Well done! Well done!"

"I am. I am," agreed the happy dragon. "It's easy, once you know how." And he blew out a great blazing gust of flames. Once he had started he blew and snorted, snuffled and sneezed as if his nose were so full of fire he couldn't get rid of enough of it.

Great Smould edged towards the cage, but the iron bars began to glow and bend and he couldn't touch them.

"You're free, little friend," cried Manon, struggling to escape from Lady Bolda, "just push your way out."

"Oh no you don't," growled Lady Bolda. She let go of Manon and ran at the cage, but the flames grilled her nose and she hopped away, screaming.

The dragon's child put his head through the melting bars, scarcely feeling their burning heat. Next came his shoulders.

"Come on," urged Manon.

The dragon's child wriggled and pushed and, with a fiery snort, he leapt out of the cage.

"Got you!" Great Smould pounced on the dragon, missing by inches. "After him," he yelled, as Dando rushed to freedom.

The Welkin people took no notice of their leader. This time they weren't interested in the flight of a fabulous beast, especially one so small. They had something else to worry about; a horrible howling that made their teeth chatter, their spines tingle and their hair stand on end. It was coming from the forest.

Doggins

"Run! Run! Run!" cried Manon.

The Welkin people were staring at the trees in horror and hardly noticed Dando racing through their midst. He scampered under the bracken, out on to the cliffs and down to the sand. And then he ran from beach to beach until he found a new cave, a deep dark hidden cave, with an entrance so well concealed that only the bird's sharp eye could have seen it.

"What's the matter with you?" Great Smould roared at his people. "Are you afraid of howling. Light the torches and into the forest with you. Come on, I'll lead the way." The fabulous beast could wait a while. Great Smould wanted to know what sort of creatures were making that horrible noise.

The Welkin people felt ashamed. They were strong and fierce; they shouldn't be afraid of a noise, however terrible. They lit their torches and ran into the forest. Deeper and deeper they went, until darkness smothered the light, and the flames began to waver in the airless crush of leaves and branches. Deeper and deeper, while the howling faded to a distant wail, and at last the Welkins were almost lost in the thick dark silence of the forest. And then, in the glimmer of dying flames, Great Smould caught just one glimpse of a horrible creature before it vanished. "Doggins," he whispered. "That's what they are. I've heard stories of what they can do. Come, let's go back and make the camp fire safe."

The Welkin people hardly slept a wink that night. They took it in turns to pace round the camp, torch in hand, peering into the darkness, ready to call a warning if the doggins attacked.

But Manon was so happy to know the little dragon was free, she crept into her shelter, pulled a blanket over her eyes and fell fast asleep.

Next day the Welkin people built a stout fence round their camp, and constructed a high tower where one of them could sit all day, observing the edge of the forest. But the doggins never attacked in daylight. They crept forward at night, howling and screeching outside the fence, but never daring to go further. The Welkin people left their torches burning all night long, and the doggins kept their distance at first. They were afraid of fire.

Soon the doggins grew bolder. They would shake the fence posts, tear at the boards and thrust their long hairy arms through the wooden lattice. The Welkin people became quite worn out with anxiety and sleeplessness. They spent their days repairing the fence and trying to think of ways to stop the doggins making their lives a misery. But even Great Smould was too tired to come up with any ideas.

Weeks passed in this way, and everyone forgot about the small fabulous beast that had once caused such excitement. Everyone except Manon, Manon and one other. Lord Drum could think of nothing else. Ignoring the nightly barks and howls, he would lie awake, remembering the dread that had flickered in the eyes of the fabulous beast when he approached. And when he slept, his dreams were filled with the image of the small coppery-green creature wrapped in Manon's arms.

A few days after the dragon's child escaped, the bird led Manon to his new hidden cave. And she visited him nearly every day. The Welkin people were too preoccupied to notice when she raided their store rooms, and she was able to take the dragon dried fish, salt pork, corn bread, fruit, biscuits, cakes and vegetables. All sorts of delicious and nourishing food found its way into Dando's secret cave. He could eat almost anything, and his appetite was enormous.

After a while Manon began to notice a change in the dragon's child. His delicate copper-green wings turned a shade darker. The spines on his back hardened into spiky triangles that pricked her hands when she tried to stroke him. Very soon it became impossible to put both arms around the dragon's neck. He had grown too big. And his welcoming grunts were now accompanied by tiny sparks that stung Manon's cheeks.

One day, when Manon slipped out of the store room with a bucket of corn, she found Lord Drum barring her way. "I've been watching you," he said. "You've been stealing our food." Manon glared at Lord Drum. "I'm hungry," she said. "And it isn't stealing. I work hard for what I get."

"But it's not for you, is it?" Lord Drum plunged his hand into the bucket and brought out a fistful of corn. "It's for the fabulous beast, I know it is. Can't he catch his own food yet?"

"It's none of your business," snapped Manon.

"Yes, it is. He belongs to me. I caught him."

"He doesn't belong to anyone," Manon declared. "And you'll never, ever see him again."

"I'll follow you," said Lord Drum. "And I'll find out where he's hiding."

Manon dropped her bucket. "You'll be sorry if you do," she said in a low whisper. "Once you nearly killed him, but you can't hurt him now, he's grown too big. And if you come anywhere near him, he'll fry you to a cinder."

To Manon's surprise Lord Drum didn't argue. He took a step backwards, letting the corn trickle through his fingers. "Will he always hate me?" he asked with a catch in his voice.

"Who knows?" said Manon, and she pushed past the boy with a scowl that made him wish he'd never asked her.

To make sure she wasn't followed, Manon took a different route to the dragon's cave that day. Every now and then she stopped and glanced over her shoulder, but Lord Drum was too quick for her. He always managed to duck behind a tree or a bush or a boulder. And in this way, he followed Manon all the way down to a small secluded beach that he had never seen before.

When he saw Manon slip behind the tall grey rock that hid the dragon's cave, Lord Drum hung back, afraid of what the dragon might do to him. And something in the air made him shiver, a feeling of unease. But sounds beyond the steep white cliffs were muffled and remote. Howls and cries were nothing more than a distant whine, like wind sighing through the bracken.

How could Lord Drum have known that the doggins, braving daylight at last, were at that very moment, climbing into the Welkins' camp?

The Biggest Drum in the World

The dragon's cave was beginning to give off rather a bad smell. "You spend too much time in here," Manon told Dando. "Come into the sun."

But Dando had nightmares about the weeks he'd spent in a cage, and he was frightened of being caught again. He only felt safe outside when the light was fading. "I'd rather not come out yet," he said.

"It's getting smelly in here," Manon scolded. "You need fresh air, come to that so do I," she pinched her nose. "And apart from anything else you need more room to practise flying."

"I suppose I do." Dando went to the mouth of the cave and cautiously poked out his head. Manon gave him a little push and he shuffled into the sunshine. It was such a beautiful day, for a while Dando forgot to be frightened, and soon they were leaping over the fine bubbles that sparkled at the edge of the sea. Every now and then Dando would spread his wings and sweep them through the spray, covering Manon with a glittering cascade of water. And although she was laughing, Manon was stunned by the great curve of the dragon's wings, and the length of fine bones that held the membrane of shimmering golden scales. So why couldn't Dando fly? Was he lazy? Or afraid of falling?

From his hiding place on the cliff, Lord Drum watched Manon and the dragon, longing to be with them, and desperately wishing that he were not a Welkin child.

When the sun was at its fiercest, and they stood in their own shadows, Manon said goodbye to Dando and ran back to the camp before she could be missed. As she approached the tall fence she wondered at the eerie silence. Perhaps the sun has sent everyone to sleep, she thought.

But there was no one in the camp. She looked in every shelter, even in the grand pavilion. The place was deserted. Where had the Welkin people gone? Manon didn't like them, but they were the only family she had, and she was curious to know what had become of them. Could they be in the forest collecting wood for a new building? Manon went to investigate. Doggins sleep all day, she told herself, so I'll be quite safe.

It was pleasantly cool under the tall trees, but so quiet; even the birds had stopped singing. Manon walked deeper and deeper into the forest. As she walked on she never dreamt that the Welkin people were far, far away. They had run to hide in the distant hills when the camp was invaded by doggins. And where were the doggins now?

The trees that crowded round Manon were so tall and dense, they turned day into night. Only a stray sunbeam managed to pierce the thick canopy of leaves. And all at once, Manon realised that she had lost the path. She turned round, again and again, searching for a landmark, for anything that might show her the way out. She saw a light, two lights, red pinpoints of flame that multiplied as they drew closer. Ten, twelve, twenty. And now Manon could see that the lights were glowing fiery eyes, and she screamed in a voice she hadn't used since the day the Welkins had captured her.

High above, the bird's sharp eyes had marked Manon's passage through the trees, and hearing the desperate cry, she guessed what had happened. "Doggins!" she twittered, and she swung down to the beach and the dragon's cave as fast as she could.

"Dragon's child!" screamed the bird, waking Dando from a pleasant sleep on his latest favourite rock. "Come quickly! Manon needs us. She's in the forest, and there are doggins everywhere."

"Oh! Oh! Oh!" Dando tumbled off the rock. "Doggins? What shall we do? What *can* we do?"

"How should I know?" cried the bird. "You think of something for a change."

Dando couldn't think. There wasn't time to think. His head was buzzing. He tore up the cliff path, while the bird flew before him, across the field of bracken, round the empty camp and into the forest. And when he saw the doggins' fiery lamp-like eyes, he forgot to be frightened and became very, very angry. "Don't you dare hurt my friend," he breathed. "Don't you dare!" And his breath was filled with burning sparks that made the nasty creatures shrink back, howling in dismay.

"This way! This way!" sang the bird, looping over the long, hairy arms that reached out to catch her.

At last the two friends burst into the

little clearing where Manon stood, too terrified to scream anymore. Dando rushed to her side. "Climb on my back," he commanded, "and we'll fly away."

Manon scrambled onto the rough back and clasped one of Dando's horny spines.

"Dando," she whispered. "Can you really fly?"

"I'll have to," he grunted. "It's now or never," and with a beating heart he remembered his mother's instructions. "Think flying! Let your thoughts run into your wings." And so he did. He thought and thought, he tried and tried. His beautiful golden wings brushed the forest floor and fanned the dark forest air, scattering dust into the narrow rays of sunlight, but they wouldn't lift him off the ground. Two glistening tears spilled from his beautiful golden eyes as he said in a hushed voice, "My wings are useless. I shall never fly."

Manon laid her head against the scaly back. "You will," she whispered, "for you are marvellous and magical. You just need a little time."

Time. Yes, that was it. He needed time to get his wings into the right rhythm. But there was no time left. The doggins, sensing victory, had begun to creep closer. Soon they lost all fear of the helpless dragon, and were running round him, shrieking with laughter, and leaping through the angry bursts of flame as if they were nothing more than moonbeams.

Manon began to lose hope. She closed her eyes and waited for a sharp claw to drag her from the dragon's back. But, all at once, the terrible shrieking stopped,

92

and into the sudden silence there came a distant, 'Boom! Boom! Boom!' Closer and closer. 'Boom! Boom! Boom!'

Manon opened her eyes. There, only a few feet away, stood Lord Drum. He had made himself a new drum, it looked like the biggest drum in the world, and it made a deep, threatening sound. 'Boom! Boom! Boom!'

The doggins shrank back, stupefied by the drumming. To their ears it was a strange and dreadful noise. It bit into their skulls and crushed their thoughts. 'Boom! Boom! Boom!' They covered their ears and tried to shake the drumming out of their heads.

"Fly, fabulous beast, while you still have time!" called Lord Drum.

Dando dipped his wings; his toes bit into the ground and pushed. The golden wings swept upwards, lifting Dando into the air.

"Up here!" called the bird, and Dando tilted towards a tiny patch of blue, where the giant trees parted to reveal the sky.

But Manon, looking back, saw brave Lord Drum, still beating a rhythm on his giant drum. He looked up with a pale, determined face and smiled at her. And Manon found that she couldn't leave him.

"We must take Lord Drum," she said, "the doggins will eat him, and he saved our lives."

"In that case . . ." agreed Dando, and he swooped towards the boy while Manon shouted, "Jump, Lord Drum. Catch hold of the dragon's tail."

"A dragon," said Lord Drum. "So that's what he is," and casting his drumsticks aside, he leapt for the dragon's tail.

Up they soared, up, up and up. While the doggins howled in fury. Up above the trees, and into the warm bright sky.

"Where are we going?" called Manon.

"Where all dragons go," sang Dando. "We're going to the Homeland."

"Since you're going my way," the bird settled on the dragon's head, "I might as well grab a lift."

The Welkin people looked up in astonishment as Dando sailed over their heads, a bird on his crest, a girl on his back, and a boy, sitting on his tail.

"It's the fabulous beast," cried Lady Bolda, "and he's stealing our son."

"Perhaps the beast is saving our son," murmured her husband, and he watched the great winged creature flying north, until he was no bigger than a speck of glittering, windblown dust. And Great Smould felt a terrible emptiness when he saw his only son, the last Welkin child, disappear. Perhaps he wouldn't have felt so bad if he'd known how happy Lord Drum would be in the dragons' Homeland.

In time the World forgot about doggins and the Welkin people. It was just as if they had never existed.

But, of course, no one ever forgot about dragons.